THE BOX BOYS

AND THE FAIRGROUND RIDE

THE BOX BOYS
AND THE FAIRGROUND RIDE

Jenny Nimmo

Illustrated by Anthony Lewis

Hodder
Children's
Books

a division of Hodder Headline

A Catalogue record for this book is available from the British
Library

ISBN 0 340 73291 1

Printed and bound in Great Britain by Guernsey Press,
Guernsey, Channel Islands

Hodder Children's Books
a division of Hodder Headline
338 Euston Road
London NW1 3BH

For the children and staff of
Buttington County Primary School

Chapter One

"The Fair's come to town!"
Scott Box jumped over the low
wall and ran up to a window.
He could see his friend, John,
watching TV in the living room.

John's dog, Bunk, was watching
TV, too.

Scott rapped on the window.
"John, can't you hear me?"
Bunk started barking and John
turned and looked over his
shoulder. He saw Scott and ran

to open the window. "What did you say?"

"There's a fair in town. They're setting it up right now.

We could go tomorrow. It's Saturday."

"A fair?" John looked puzzled. "What sort of fair?"

He thought of Church Fairs
and School Book Fairs.

"You know, with swingboats,
and roundabouts and ghost-
trains and coconut-shys and
goldfish in jars."

"Oh, wow!" John suddenly
remembered the fair last
Christmas.

"When shall we go?"

"Tomorrow – my dad said he'd take us."

"Yesss! Yesss! Come in and help me count my pocket money." John rushed to open the door and Scott came bouncing in.

"Who's there?" called John's mum from the kitchen.

"Scott," said John. "His dad's taking us to the fairground tomorrow. We're just going to count my money now."

"I'll give you a bit extra," said his mum. "If you're good."

John emptied his piggy bank on to the living-room carpet.

Silver and copper coins rolled across the floor. Scott crawled after them, while John began to count. It took him quite a long time because Bunk kept jumping on the coins.

"Six pounds and fifty-seven pence," John said at last.

"Plenty," said Scott. "I've got five pounds and Dad said he'd give me another five. We can have a go on just about everything."

"I wonder . . ." said John. "I wonder if anything special will happen?"

Scott knew what John meant.
They looked at each other,
wondering.

There was
something
rather special
about John and
Scott. Something
strange.
Several things, in fact.
Scott and John
had the same
surname: Box.
They were
also born on the
same day in the
same year, and they
lived in the same street.

They didn't look like each
other but they did like doing
the same things. They even
liked the same food and the
same TV programmes.

Everyone called them the 'Box
Boys', and they were always
together.

Because it was unusual to have the same name *and* to be born at the same time, John and Scott often wondered if something unusual would happen to them. Scott had a feeling that it might happen in the fairground. After all, a fairground is a rather magical place, the sort of place where anything could happen. John's mother called, "Come and have your tea," and John put his money back into the china pig.

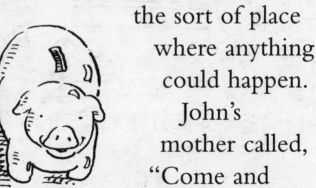

"I'd better go," said Scott.
"See you tomorrow!"

"What time?" asked John.

"Dad said in the evening
when it's getting dark and all
the coloured lights are on!"

"Great!"

17

Chapter Two

The next evening after tea, John
stood waiting at the window.
It was early spring and still dark
and cold in the evenings. John's
mum had made him wear a hat,

but John didn't mind because
the hat had alien faces on it.

Scott came leaping up the
path while his mum and dad
waited at the gate. Scott wore a
scarf that matched John's hat;
they always tried to wear the
same sort of clothes.

"They're here, Mum!" cried John.

Mrs Box came to the door with him. She put five pound coins in his hand and told him to have fun. Bunk wanted to go to the fair, too, but Mrs Box said, "No, Bunk!

Fairgrounds are dangerous for dogs."

Scott and John raced each
other to the gate, then they piled
into the car behind Scott's mum
and dad, and off they went.

The fair had been set up on a
big field just outside the town.
They could see the lights
strung out across the sky like
coloured stars, and as they
drove nearer they could hear
the music.

All sorts of music, tunes jumbled together, now loud now soft – songs echoed across the fields like voices from another world.

"This must be the place," Scott whispered to John, "the place where something will happen. Can't you feel it?"

"Not yet," said John.

They parked in a field beside the fairground and as soon as John stepped out of the car he could feel it. It was just like Scott said. Something was going to happen.

They wandered through the crowds, trying to decide where to start. There were so many stalls.

Scott's dad had a go on the rifle-range and won a pink teddy bear. Scott and John shook their heads when he offered it to them.

"If only it had been a dinosaur," said Scott.

Scott's mum said, "I've always wanted a pink teddy bear, I'll have it." She tucked the bear in the crook of her arm, where it looked very happy.

John and Scott tried to get a goldfish next, but they just couldn't seem to get the Ping-Pong balls in the jars.

Neither could Scott's mum and dad. To cheer themselves up they went to the candyfloss stall. Scott ended up with candyfloss on his eyebrows. John had a long pink beard.

"You look like old men," laughed Scott's dad.

Next they went on the
roller-coaster.

Holding tight to the bars of
their carriage they rumbled up
into the sky, then down again,
faster and faster, everyone
screaming so loud that the Box
Boys couldn't hear their own
voices.

"I want to go on the ghost train," said Scott, when they were safely back on land.

Scott's mum shook her head. "It'll give me nightmares," she said, "and I'm not letting you two go alone."

"Pleeaase!" begged the Box Boys, looking at Scott's dad.

"Look at the queue," he said. "You'll be waiting all night. How about the dodgems?"

"Yeesss!" yelled the Box Boys.

John chose a red car, Scott chose yellow.

"This is the best thing of all," Scott shouted as he bumped

and banged his way around the
other cars.

But it wasn't so good when a
red-haired boy started driving
into him. *Bang! Bang! Bang!*

Scott was looking worried so
John came to the rescue and
bumped the red-haired boy
from behind.

The boy whizzed round with
a shout, but before he could
bump John back the power
died and the cars all came to a
standstill.

The red-haired boy ran off
into the crowd and someone
shouted, "Here comes trouble.
What've you been up to, Pete?"
"What shall we do
next?" asked Scott.
John couldn't
make up his mind.
And then he saw
the roundabout.

"Look!" he pointed
at the flying
animals: horses,
elephants, giraffes,
dolphins, bears
and dragons, all
swooping round in
time to the music.

Scott had a funny feeling in
the pit of his stomach. He
stared at the animals leaping
round and round.

They almost looked real as
they began to move faster; like
running, galloping, lolloping,
leaping wild animals.

There were more mums and dads than children riding the roundabout creatures.

"D'you want to have a ride?" Scott asked his mum and dad.

"We'll watch," said Mrs Box, "just to make sure nothing happens."

"What could happen?" asked John, all at once a bit scared.

"Well . . . anything, I suppose," said Mrs Box. "You never know. Just hold on tight."

"Anything could happen," murmured Scott. "I wonder what will happen?"

Chapter Three

When the roundabout stopped
the riders got off and the Box
Boys stepped up to claim their
animals. John chose an
elephant. Scott chose a giraffe.

Almost as soon as the music
started again the Box Boys
knew something strange was
about to occur. The painted
animals seemed to be made of
real skin and bone!

John could feel muscles rippling under him; the paint on his elephant felt like hard, leathery skin. He closed his eyes and clung tightly to the pole that held his elephant to the roundabout.

Now they were going faster and faster.

The music seemed jumbled with other sounds: wind, water, crackling branches and running feet. Gone were the fairground scents of candyfloss, burgers, metal and oil.

All John could smell was a strange mixture of leaves and animals. A wild, jungly, foreign smell. He dared not open his eyes.

"John," someone whispered. Was it Scott? "John, look! Look!"

John didn't dare open his
eyes.

Suddenly the animal beneath
him tripped and lurched
forward. John's eyes flew open.

What had happened? All he
could see for miles and miles
was dry golden-brown earth.

Here and there scrubby-looking trees sprouted out of the ground; a few patches of brush and dry grass grew in their shade, but very little else.

John seemed to be lying on something: a moving grey-brown, leathery back. What could it be? He turned his head and found a great shape towering beside him.

Shading his eyes against the sun, John gazed up at the huge form. There was another beyond it, and another behind it.

They were elephants. Great, tusky, African elephants. And John seemed to be astride a baby elephant.

"Where am I?" John gasped.

"Hi!" called a voice. "John, John!" The voice seemed to be coming from a big dust cloud a few metres away.

As John stared at the cloud a small giraffe came galloping into view. Scott was sitting on the giraffe's back.

"I think we're in Africa," said Scott. "Isn't it great!"

"Brilliant," said John. "But how did we get here? And what's that?" He pointed to a huge, ugly-looking bird sitting on top of a scrubby tree.

"It's a vulture," said Scott.

"They eat dead things."

"Ugh!" John shivered.

All at once the vulture spread its great wings and swept into the sky.

This seemed to frighten the giraffe. It turned and galloped away with Scott clinging to its neck.

"Scott! Scott! Come back!" yelled John.

The elephants began to pick up speed.

Now they were running. John was surprised at how fast an elephant could run. He'd always thought of them as slow and clumsy.

He clung to the top of the baby elephant's ears, but still he slipped and slid around on the leathery back. With a sudden cry, John lost his grip and fell to the ground, while a forest of giant limbs thundered past him.

If one great foot trod on any part of him, he'd be finished.

John didn't know whether to keep very still or to try and crawl away. He decided to stay where he was until all the elephants had gone. When the last great beast seemed to have passed, he lifted his head and looked back to see if he was safe.

He wasn't.

There was something much worse than an elephant behind him. Much more dangerous. Two hungry-looking lions were standing only a few metres away. They were staring straight at John with fierce golden eyes.

John held his breath. If he moved, he knew the lions would catch him in a second.

There was nowhere to run. Nowhere to hide.

One of the lions lowered its head and began to move towards him, like a cat stalking a mouse. The other lion followed. Then they broke into a run and John covered his eyes.

Chapter Four

"Hey! Hey!" It was Scott's voice.
John uncovered his eyes and
looked up. The lions, distracted
by this voice, were both
watching a giraffe racing past the

herd of elephants.

"It's OK, John," Scott called.
"I think the lions are coming
after me."

"But . . ." Before John could
say another word he
was lifted off the
ground by a
long grey
trunk. As
he hung
there, high
in the air,
he saw herds
of terrified
animals
running from the
lions' roar.

"Watch out!" John called
back to Scott.

"Don't worry, the elephants
are going to help," yelled Scott.

He was right. As John's
rescuer lifted him gently over
her head, he saw that the other
elephants were coming back.
Below him a huge wall began
to form. A wall of moving,
shoving, shuffling elephants.

They lifted their trunks and shrieked at the lions, daring them to attack.

The lions knew they were beaten. With one last snarl, they turned and slunk into the undergrowth.

Still clasped in the elephant's trunk, John found himself swinging down to the ground. Down, down, down until the elephant let go and John dropped on to the dry earth.

Everything had gone very quiet. The running animals had

kicked up so much dust that
John could hardly see a thing.

But as the dust began to settle
he could make out a shape,
lying beside him. The shape
moaned.

"Ooh! I feel
bruised all
over." It
was Scott.
"I fell off,"
he said.

"The
animals have
gone," John told
him. "All of them. Look!"

Scott sat up. "How are we
going to get home?" he said.
"Without our animals?"

The adventure didn't seem so much fun now.

"Don't know," said John. But even as he spoke he noticed two familiar forms lying beneath a tree. An elephant and a giraffe. They were both fast asleep.

"Look!" said John.

The boys picked themselves
up and ran to the animals. John
scrambled on to the elephant
and Scott climbed on to the
giraffe. "Wake up! Wake up!"
the boys shouted.

The animals lifted their heads
and slowly got to their feet.
And then they took off.

They rans so fast that the Box
Boys began to feel dizzy.

The elephant and the giraffe
ran in a circle.

Round and round and round.
Music seeped into the boys' ears
and the sharp smell of animals
became the familiar sweet and
sour tang of the fairground.

Now John
could see lights
all around him;
red, green,
yellow and blue,
glittering against
a night sky.

And there, behind
him, was Scott.
The boys were
moving up and
down on their
wooden animals.

58

John stared at Scott and Scott stared back. He leaned closer to John's fairground elephant and shouted above the music, "That was great!"

"Yes," said
John, "but
I'm glad
we're
back."
The
music
died and the
roundabout stopped.

As they climbed off their animals, John found that his legs weren't doing exactly what he wanted them to.

He swayed this way and that, still feeling dizzy. He noticed that Scott was doing the same. They laughed at each other.

Scott's mum and dad ran to meet them.

"That must have been a good ride," said Scott's dad. "You went so fast we could hardly see you."

"Too fast," said Scott's mum. She frowned and looked hard at Scott's head. "There's sand in your hair," she said. "Wherever did that come from?"

For a moment Scott didn't
know how to answer her. Then
he said, "We've been on safari."

"On safari?" Scott's mum
looked puzzled.

"You said anything could
happen, Mum,"
Scott reminded
her.

His dad
began to
laugh. "Of
course! An
elephant and a
giraffe. I suppose
you've been to Africa
– that's why we couldn't see
you."

The Box Boys nodded. They
were too tired to have any more
rides. Too tired even to try for a
goldfish again. But as they were
leaving the fairground, Scott's
dad decided to have one last go.
His Ping-Pong ball went
straight into the
goldfish jar.
  "There," he
said. "I knew
it was my
lucky day!
Who wants a
goldfish?"
  John looked back at
the roundabout. It looked so
magical.

He wondered if the elephant had come alive again and was carrying its rider through Africa. No, he decided. That could only happen to a Box Boy.

"I'll have the goldfish," said Scott. "I think John would rather have an elephant."

The Box Boys grinned at each other.

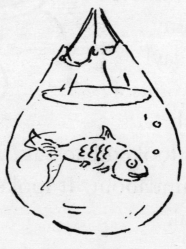